Dear parents, caregivers, and educators:

If you want to get your child excited about reading, you've come to the right place! Ready-to-Read *GRAPHICS* is the perfect launchpad for emerging graphic novel readers.

All Ready-to-Read *GRAPHICS* books include the following:

★ **A how-to guide to reading graphic novels for first-time readers**

★ **Easy-to-follow panels to support reading comprehension**

★ **Accessible vocabulary to build your child's reading confidence**

★ **Compelling stories that star your child's favorite characters**

★ **Fresh, engaging illustrations that provide context and promote visual literacy**

Wherever your child may be on their reading journey, Ready-to-Read *GRAPHICS* will make them giggle, gasp, and want to keep reading more.

Blast off on this starry adventure . . . a universe of graphic novel reading awaits!

Figgy & Boone

Best Brother EVER!

written and illustrated by
Janee Trasler

Ready-to-Read *GRAPHICS*

SIMON SPOTLIGHT

An imprint of Simon & Schuster Children's Publishing Division • New York London Toronto Sydney New Delhi
1230 Avenue of the Americas, New York, New York 10020
This Simon Spotlight edition September 2022 • Copyright © 2022 by Janee Trasler • All rights reserved, including the right of reproduction in whole or in part in any form.
SIMON SPOTLIGHT, READY-TO-READ, and colophon are registered trademarks of Simon & Schuster, Inc. • For information about special discounts for bulk purchases,
please contact Simon & Schuster Special Sales at 1-866-506-1949 or business@simonandschuster.com. • Manufactured in China 0522 SCP
1 3 5 7 9 10 8 6 4 2
This book has been cataloged with the Library of Congress.
ISBN 978-1-6659-1449-9 (hc)
ISBN 978-1-6659-1448-2 (pbk)
ISBN 978-1-6659-1450-5 (ebook)

How to Read This Book

This is Figgy. He's here to give you some tips on reading this book.

It's me, Figgy! The pointy end of this speech bubble shows that I'm speaking.

When someone is thinking, you'll see a bubbly cloud with little circles pointing to them.

This box I'm inside is called a panel. On each page, read the panels from left to right...

...and top to bottom.

Hooray!

Now you're READY TO READ this book!

purr... purr...

Those purrs are the sound of a cat nearby. I had better get going!

CONTENTS

Chapter 1

Best Brother

Boone, you're the best brother ever.

Brothers.

Not brothers.

But I made
a family album.

Gasp!

Boone's Guide to Common Rodents

rat

mouse

hamster

gerbil

guinea pig

Figgy's Family Album

me

my brother
Boone

Chapter 2
Next Brother

I found my brother.

That is not your brother, Figgy.

He's not?

No. He also belongs to a different species.

Huh?

He's a hamster.

Hamsters and mice are not brothers.

Cousins?

21

Figgy's Family Album

me

my brother
Boone

cousin Hammie

27

Figgy, that is a stink bug.

Sniff

Bye, bug!

Figgy's Family Album

cousin Lizzy

cousin Gerb

cousin Stinky

me

cousin Piggie

my brother Boone

cousin Dolly

cousin Hammie

cousin Turtle

Boone's Guide to the Food Chain

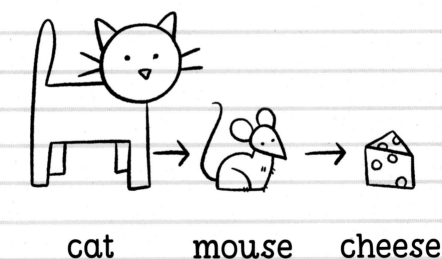

cat   mouse   cheese

Figgy's Favorite Foods

cheese

cheesy
puff

cheesy
noodles

cheesy
toast

cheesy
crackers

cheese
pizza

cheesecake

Chapter 3
Oh Brother

44

Whew. That was close, Boone.

You can say that again.

That was close, Boone.

You heard me.
Let him go.

THUMP

Bye, Cat.